# Room for the
# Young Dead

**Faber
Stories**

The French-Czech novelist Milan Kundera was born in the Czech Republic and has lived in France since 1975. He is the author of the internationally acclaimed and bestselling novels *The Joke*, *Life is Elsewhere*, *The Farewell Waltz*, *The Book of Laughter and Forgetting*, *The Unbearable Lightness of Being* and *Immortality*, and the short-story collection *Laughable Loves* – all originally in Czech. His more recent novels, *Slowness*, *Identity* and *Ignorance*, as well as his non-fiction works, *The Art of the Novel*, *Testaments Betrayed*, *The Curtain* and *Encounter*, were originally written in French.

# Milan Kundera

# Let the Old Dead Make Room for the Young Dead

Faber Stories

ff

First published in this edition in 2019
by Faber & Faber Limited
Bloomsbury House
74–77 Great Russell Street
London WC1B 3DA
First published in English in *Laughable Loves* in 1974

Typeset by Faber & Faber Limited
Printed and bound by CPI Group (UK) Ltd, Croydon, CR0 4YY

A CIP record for this book
is available from the British Library

ISBN 978–0–571–35690–4

10 9 8 7 6 5 4 3 2 1

# 1

He was returning home along the street of a small Bohemian town, where he had been living for several years, reconciled to his not-too-exciting life, his backbiting neighbours, and the monotonous rowdiness that surrounded him at work, and he was walking so totally without seeing (as one walks along a path traversed a hundred times) that he almost passed her by. But she had already recognised him from a distance, and coming towards him she gave him that gentle smile of hers; only at the last moment, when they had almost passed each other, did the smile ring a bell in his memory and snap him out of his drowsy state.

'I wouldn't have recognised you!' he apologised, but it was an awkward apology, because it brought them precipitously to a painful subject, about which it would have been advisable to keep silent; they had not seen each other for fifteen years and during this time they had both aged. 'Have I changed so much?' she asked, and he replied that she hadn't, and even if this was a lie it wasn't an out-and-out lie, because that gentle smile (expressing demurely and restrainedly a capacity for some sort of eternal enthusiasm) emerged from the distance of many years quite unchanged, and it confused him: it evoked for him so distinctly the former appearance of this woman that he had to make a definite effort to disregard it and to see her as she was now: she was almost an old woman.

He asked her where she was going and what was on her schedule, and she replied that she had nothing else to do but wait for the train that would take her back to Prague that evening. He evinced pleasure at their unexpected meeting, and because they agreed (with good reason) that the two local cafés were overcrowded and dirty, he invited her to his bachelor apartment, which wasn't very far away; he had both coffee and tea there, and, more important, it was clean and peaceful.

# 2

Right from the start it had been a bad day. Her husband (twenty-five years ago she had lived here with him for a short time as a new bride, then they had moved to Prague, where he'd died ten years back) was buried, thanks to an eccentric wish in his last will and testament, in the local cemetery. At that time she had paid in advance for a ten-year lease on the grave, but a few days before, she had become afraid that the time limit had expired and that she had forgotten to renew the lease. Her first impulse had been to write the cemetery administration, but then she had realised how futile it was to correspond with the authorities, and she had come out here.

She knew the path to her husband's grave from memory, and yet today she felt all as if she was in this cemetery for the first time. She couldn't find the grave, and it seemed to her that she had gone astray. It took her a while to understand. There, where the grey sandstone monument with the name of her husband in gold lettering used to be, precisely on that spot (she confidently recognised the two neighbouring graves) now stood a black marble headstone with a quite different name in gilt.

Upset, she went to the cemetery administration. There they told her that upon expiration of the leases, the graves were cancelled. She reproached them for not have advised her that she should renew the lease, and they replied that there was little room in the cemetery and that *the old dead must make room for the young dead*. This exasperated her, and she told them, holding back her tears, that they knew absolutely nothing of human dignity or respect for others, but she understood that the conversation was useless. Just as she could not have prevented her husband's death, so also she was defenseless against his second death, this death of an *old dead* who is now forbidden to exist even as dead.

She went off into town, and anxiety quickly began to mingle with her sorrow as she tried to imagine how she would explain to her son the disappearance of his father's grave and how she would justify her neglect. At last fatigue overtook her: she didn't know how to pass the long hours until time for the departure of her train, for she no longer knew anyone here, and nothing encouraged her to take even a sentimental stroll, because over the years the town had changed too much, and the once familiar places looked quite strange to her now. That is why she gratefully accepted the invitation of the (half-forgotten) old acquaintance she'd met by chance: She could wash her hands in his bathroom and then sit in his soft armchair (her legs ached), look around his room, and listen to the boiling water bubbling away behind the screen that separated the kitchen nook from the room.

# 3

Not long ago he had turned thirty-five, and exactly at that time he had noticed that the hair on top of his head was thinning very visibly. The bald spot wasn't there yet, but its appearance was quite conceivable (the scalp was showing beneath the hair) and, more important, it was certain to appear and in the not-too-distant future. Certainly it was ridiculous to make thinning hair a matter of life or death, but he realised that baldness would change his face and that his hitherto youthful appearance (undeniably his best) was on its way out.

And now these considerations made him think about how the balance sheet of this person (with hair), who was going away bit by bit, actually stood, what he had actually experienced and enjoyed. What astounded him was the knowledge that he had experienced rather little; when he thought about this he felt embarrassed; yes, he was ashamed, because to live here on earth so long and to experience so little was ignominious.

What did he actually mean when he said to himself that he had not experienced much? Did he mean by this travel, work, public service, sports, women? Of course he meant all of these things; yet, above all, women; because if his life was deficient in other spheres it certainly upset him, but he didn't have to lay the blame for it on himself; anyhow, not for work that was uninteresting and without prospects; not for curtailing his travels because he didn't have money or reliable party references; finally, not even for the fact that when he was twenty he had injured his knee and had had to give up sports, which he had enjoyed. On the other hand, the realm of women was for him a sphere of relative freedom, and that being so, he couldn't make any excuses about it; here he could have demonstrated his wealth; women became for him the one legitimate criterion of life's *density*.

But no such luck! Things had gone somewhat badly for him with women: Until he was twenty-five (though he was a good-looking guy) shyness would tie him up in knots; then he fell in love, got married, and after seven years had persuaded himself that it was possible to find the infinity of erotic possibilities in one woman; then he got divorced and the one-woman apologetics (and the illusion of infinity) melted away, and in their place came an agreeable taste for and boldness in the pursuit of women (a pursuit of their varied finiteness); unfortunately his bad financial situation frustrated his newfound desires (he had to pay his former wife for the support of a child he was allowed to see once or twice a year), and conditions in the small town were such that the curiosity of the neighbours was as enormous as the choice of women was scant.

And time was already passing very quickly, and all at once he was standing in the bathroom in front of the oval mirror located above the washbasin; in his right hand he held over his head a round mirror and was transfixed examining the bald spot that had begun to appear; this sight suddenly (without preparation) brought home to him the banal truth that what he'd missed couldn't be made good. He found himself in a state of chronic ill humour and was even assailed by thoughts of suicide. Naturally (and it is necessary to emphasise this, in order not to see him as a hysterical or stupid person), he appreciated the comic aspects of these thoughts, and he knew that he would never carry them out (he laughed inwardly at his own suicide note: *I won't put up with my bald spot. Farewell!*), but it is enough that these thoughts, however platonic they may have been, assailed him at all. Let us try to understand: the thoughts made themselves felt within him perhaps as the overwhelming desire to give up the race makes itself felt within a marathon runner, when halfway through he discovers that shamefully (and moreover through his own fault, his own blunders) he is losing. He also considered his race lost, and he didn't feel like running any farther.

And now he bent down over the small table and placed one cup of coffee on it in front of the couch (on which he was going to sit down), the other in front of the armchair, in which his visitor was sitting, and said to himself that there was a strange spitefulness

9

in the fact that he had encountered this woman, with whom he had once been madly in love and whom he had allowed to escape him (through his own fault), encountered her precisely when he found himself in this state of mind and at a time when it was no longer possible to recapture anything.

# 4

She would hardly have guessed that in his eyes she was *the one who had escaped him*; still, she had always remembered the night they had spent together; she remembered how he had looked then (he was twenty, didn't know how to dress, used to blush, and his boyishness amused her); and she remembered what she had been like (she had been almost forty, and a thirst for beauty drove her into the arms of other men, but also drove her away from them; she had always thought that her life should have resembled a *delightful ball*, and she feared that her unfaithfulness to her husband might turn into an ugly habit).

Yes, she had decreed beauty for herself, as people decree moral injunctions for themselves; if she had noticed any ugliness in her own life, she would perhaps have fallen into despair. And because she was now aware that after fifteen years she must seem old to her host (with all the ugliness that this brings with it), she wanted quickly to unfold an imaginary fan in front of her face, and to this end she deluged him with questions: she asked him how he had come to this town; she asked him about his job; she complimented him on the cosiness of his bachelor apartment, and praised the view from the window over the rooftops of the town (she said that it was of course no special view, but that there was an airiness and freedom about it). She named the painters of several framed reproductions of impressionist pictures (this was not difficult, in the apartments of most poor Czech intellectuals one was certain to find these cheap prints), then she got up from the table with her unfinished cup of coffee in her hand and bent over a small writing desk, on which were a few photographs in a stand (it didn't escape her that among them there was no photo of a young woman), and she asked whether the face of the old woman in one of them belonged to his mother (he confirmed this).

Then he asked her what she had meant when she had told him earlier that she had come here to take care of some things. She really dreaded speaking about the cemetery (here on the sixth floor she not only felt high above the roofs, but also pleasantly high above her own life); when he insisted, though, she finally confessed (but very briefly, because the immodesty of hasty frankness had always been foreign to her) that she had lived here many years before, that her husband was buried here (she was silent about the cancellation of the grave), and that she and her son had been coming here for the last ten years without fail on All Souls' Day.

# 5

'Every year?' This statement saddened him, and once again he thought of the spitefulness of fate; if only he'd met her six years ago when he'd moved here, everything could have been possible; she wouldn't have been so marked by age, her appearance wouldn't have been so different from the image he had of the woman he had loved fifteen years before; it would have been within his power to surmount the difference and perceive both images (the image of the past and that of the present) as one. But now they stood hopelessly far apart.

She drank her coffee and talked. He tried hard to determine precisely the extent of the transformation by means of which she was escaping him *for the second time*: her face was wrinkled (in vain did the layer of powder try to deny this); her neck was withered (in vain did the high collar try to hide this); her cheeks sagged; her hair (but it was almost beautiful!) had grown grey; however, her hands drew his attention most of all (unfortunately, it was not possible to touch them up with powder or paint): bunches of blue veins stood out on them, so that all at once they were the hands of a man.

In him pity was mixed with anger, and he felt like drowning their too-long-put-off meeting in alcohol; he asked her if she wanted some cognac (he had an opened bottle in the cabinet behind the screen); she replied that she didn't, and he remembered that even fifteen years before she had drunk almost not at all, perhaps so that alcohol wouldn't make her behave contrary to the demands of good taste and decorum. And when he saw the delicate movement of her hand with which she refused the offer of cognac, he realised that this charm, this magic, this grace, which had enraptured him, was still the same in her, though hidden beneath the mask of old age, and was in itself still attractive, even though it was behind a grille.

When it crossed his mind that this was *the grille of age*, he felt immense pity for her, and this pity brought her nearer to him (this woman who had once been so dazzling, before whom he used to be tongue-tied), and he wanted to have a conversation with her and to talk the way a friend talks with a friend, at length, in a blue atmosphere of melancholy resignation. He started to talk (and it did indeed turn into a long talk) and eventually he got to the pessimistic thoughts that had visited him of late. Naturally he was silent about the bald spot that was beginning to appear (it was just like her silence about the cancelled grave); on the other hand the vision of the bald spot was transubstantiated into quasi-philosophical maxims to the effect that time passes more quickly than man is able to live, and that life is terrible, because everything in it is necessarily doomed to extinction; he voiced these and similar maxims, to which he awaited a sympathetic response; but he didn't get it.

'I don't like that kind of talk,' she said almost vehemently. 'Everything you've been saying is awfully superficial.'

# 6

She didn't like conversations about growing old or dying, because they contained images of physical ugliness, which went against the grain with her. Several times, almost in a fluster, she repeated to her host that his opinions were *superficial*; after all, she said, a man is more than just a body that wastes away, a man's work is substantial and that is what he leaves behind for others. Her advocacy of this opinion wasn't new; it had first come to her aid when, thirty years earlier, she had fallen in love with her former husband, who was nineteen years older than she. She had never ceased to respect him wholeheartedly (in spite of all her infidelities, about which he either didn't know or didn't want to know), and she took pains to convince herself that her husband's intellect and importance would fully outweigh the heavy load of his years.

'What kind of work, I ask you? What kind of

work do we leave behind?' protested her host with a bitter laugh.

She didn't want to refer to her dead husband, though she firmly believed in the lasting value of everything that he had accomplished; she therefore only said that every man accomplishes something, which in itself may be most modest, but that in this and only in this is his value; then she went on to talk about herself, how she worked in a house of culture in a suburb of Prague, how she organised lectures and poetry readings; she spoke (with an excitement that seemed out of proportion to him) about 'the grateful faces' of the public; then she expatiated on how beautiful it was to have a son and to see her own features (her son looked like her) changing into the face of a man; how it was beautiful to give him everything that a mother can give a son and then to fade quietly into the background of his life.

It was not by chance that she had begun to talk about her son, because all day her son had been in her thoughts, a reproachful reminder of the morning's failure at the cemetery; it was strange; she had never let any man impose his will on her, but her own son subjugated her, and she didn't understand how. The failure at the cemetery had upset her so much today, above all because she felt guilty before him and feared his reproaches. Of course she had long suspected that her son so jealously watched over the way she honored his father's memory (it was he who insisted every All Souls' Day that they should not fail to visit the cemetery!), not so much out of love for his dead father as from a desire to usurp his mother, to assign her to a widow's proper confines. For that's how it was, even if he never voiced it and she tried hard (without success) not to know it: the idea that his mother could still have a sex life disgusted him: everything in her that remained sexual (at least in the realm of possibility and chance) disgusted him, and because the idea of sex is connected with the idea of youthfulness, he was disgusted by everything that was still youthful in her; he was no longer a child, and his mother's youthfulness (combined with the aggressiveness of her motherly care) disagreeably thwarted his relationship with girls, who had begun to interest him; he wanted to have an old mother; only from such a mother would he tolerate love, and it was only such a mother he was capable of loving. And although at times she realised that in this way he was pushing her towards the grave, she had finally submitted to him, succumbed to his pressure, and even idealised her capitulation, persuading herself that the beauty of her life consisted precisely in quietly fading out in the shadow of another life. In the name of this idealisation (without which the wrinkles on her face would have made her far more uneasy), she now conducted with such unexpected warmth this dispute with her host.

But her host suddenly leaned across the low table that stood between them, stroked her hand, and said: 'Forgive my chatter. You know that I always was an idiot.'

# 7

Their dispute didn't irritate him; on the contrary his visitor yet again confirmed her identity for him. In her protest against his pessimistic talk (wasn't this above all a protest against ugliness and bad taste?), he recognised her as the person he had once known, so her former appearance and their old adventure filled his thoughts all the more. Now he wished only that nothing destroy the intimate mood, so favourable to their conversation (for that reason he stroked her hand and called himself an idiot), and he wanted to tell her about the thing that seemed most important to him at this moment: their adventure together. For he was convinced that he had experienced something very special with her, which she didn't suspect and which he himself with difficulty would now try to put into precise words.

He no longer even remembered how they had met; apparently she sometimes came in contact with his student friends, but he remembered perfectly the out-of-the-way Prague café where they had been alone together for the first time: he had been sitting opposite her in a plush booth, depressed and silent, but at the same time thoroughly elated by her delicate hints that she was favourably disposed towards him. He had tried hard to visualise (without daring to hope for the fulfillment of these dreams) how she would look if he kissed her, undressed her, and made love to her – but he just couldn't manage it. Yes, there was something odd about it: He had tried a thousand times to imagine her in bed, but in vain. Her face kept on looking at him with its calm, gentle smile and he couldn't (even with the most dogged efforts of his imagination) distort it with the grimace of erotic ecstasy. *She absolutely escaped his imagination.*

And that was the situation, which had never since been repeated in his life. At that time he had stood face-to-face with the *unimaginable*. Obviously he was experiencing that very short period (the *paradisiac* period) when the imagination is not yet satiated by experience, has not become routine, knows little, and knows how to do little, so that the unimaginable still exists; and should the unimaginable become reality (without the mediation of the imaginable, without that narrow bridge of images), a man will be seized by panic and vertigo. Such vertigo did actually overtake him, when after several further meetings, in the course of which he hadn't resolved anything, she began to ask him in detail and with meaningful curiosity about his student room in the dormitory, so that she soon forced him to invite her there.

He had shared the little room in the dorm with another student, who for a glass of rum had promised not to return until after midnight; it bore little resemblance to his bachelor apartment of today: two metal cots, two chairs, a cupboard, a glaring, unshaded light-bulb, and frightful disorder. He tidied up the room, and at seven o'clock (it went with her refinement that she was habitually on time) she knocked on the door. It was September, and only gradually did it begin to get dark. They sat down on the edge of a cot and kissed. Then it got even darker, and he didn't want to switch on the light, because he was glad that he couldn't be seen, and hoped that the darkness would relieve the state of embarrassment in which he would find himself having to undress in front of her. (If he knew tolerably well how to unbutton women's blouses, he himself would undress in front of them with bashful haste.) This time, however, he didn't for a long time dare to undo her first button (it seemed to him that in the matter of beginning to undress there must exist some tasteful and elegant procedure, which only men who were experts knew, and he was afraid of betraying his inexperience), so that in the end she herself stood up and, asking with a smile, said: 'Shouldn't I take off this armour?' She began to undress. It was dark, however, and he saw only the shadows of her movements. He hastily undressed too and gained some confidence only when they began (thanks to her patience) to make love. He looked into her face, but in the dusk her expression entirely eluded him, and he couldn't even make out her features. He regretted that it was dark, but it seemed impossible for him to get up and move away from her at that moment to turn on the switch by the door, so vainly he went on straining his eyes. But he didn't recognise her. It seemed to him that he was making love with someone else; with someone spurious or else someone quite unreal and unindividuated.

Then she had got on top of him (he could see only her raised shadow), and moving her hips, she said something in a muffled tone, in a whisper, but it wasn't clear whether she was talking to him or to herself. He couldn't make out the words and asked her what she had said. She went on whispering, and even when he clasped her to him again, he couldn't understand what she was saying.

# 8

She listened to her host and became increasingly absorbed in details she had long ago forgotten: for instance, in those days she used to wear a pale blue summer suit, in which, they said, she looked like an inviolable angel (yes, she recalled that suit); she used to wear a large ivory comb stuck in her hair, which they said gave her a majestically old-fashioned look; at the café she always used to order tea with rum (her only alcoholic vice), and all this pleasantly carried her away from the cemetery, away from the vanished monument, away from her sore feet, away from the house of culture, and away from the reproachful eyes of her son. Ah, she thought, whatever I am today, if a bit of my youth lives on in this man's memory, I haven't lived in vain. This immediately struck her as a new corroboration of her conviction that the worth of a human being lies in the ability to extend oneself, to go outside oneself, to exist in and for other people.

She listened and didn't resist him when from time to time he stroked her hand; the stroking merged with the soothing tone of the conversation and had a disarming indefiniteness about it (for whom was it intended? for the woman *about whom* he was speaking or for the woman *to whom* he was speaking?); after all, she liked the man who was stroking her; she even said to herself that she liked him better than the young man of fifteen years ago, whose boyishness, if she remembered correctly, had been rather a nuisance.

When he, in his account, got to the moment when her moving shadow had risen above him and he had vainly endeavoured to understand her whispering, he fell silent for an instant, and she (foolishly, as if he could know those words and would want to remind her of them after so many years like some forgotten mystery) asked softly: 'And what was I saying?'

# 9

'I don't know,' he replied. He didn't know; at that time she had escaped not only his imagination but also his perceptions; she had escaped his sight and hearing. When he had switched on the light in the dormitory room, she was already dressed, everything about her was once again sleek, dazzling, perfect, and he vainly sought a connection between her face in the light and the face that a moment before he had been guessing at in the darkness. They hadn't parted yet, but he was already trying to remember her; he tried to imagine how her (unseen) face and (unseen) body had looked when they'd made love a little while before – but without success. She was still escaping his imagination.

He had made up his mind that next time he would make love to her with the light on. Only there wasn't a next time. From that day on she adroitly and tactfully avoided him. He had failed hopeless-ly, yet it wasn't clear why. They'd certainly made love beautifully, but he also knew how impossible he had been *beforehand*, and he was ashamed of this; he felt condemned by her avoidance and no longer dared to pursue her.

'Tell me, why did you avoid me then?'

'I beg you,' she said in the gentlest of voices. 'It was so long ago that I don't know.' And when he pressed her further she protested: 'You shouldn't always return to the past. It's enough that we have to devote so much time to it against our will.' She said this only to ward off his insistence (and perhaps the last sentence, spoken with a light sigh, referred to her morning visit to the cemetery), but he perceived her statement differently: as an intense and purposeful clarification for him of the fact (this obvious thing) that there were not two women (from the past and from the present), but only one and the same woman, and that she, who had escaped him fifteen years earlier, was here now, was within reach of his hand.

'You're right, the present is more important,' he said in a meaningful tone, and he looked intently at her face. She was smiling with her mouth half open, and he glimpsed a row of white teeth. At that instant a recollection flashed through his head: that time in his dorm room she had put his fingers into her mouth and bitten them hard until it had hurt. Meanwhile he had been feeling the whole inside of her mouth, and he distinctly remembered that on one side at the back her upper teeth were missing (this had not disgusted him at the time; on the contrary such a trivial imperfection went with her age, which attracted and aroused him). But now, looking into the space between her teeth and the corner of her mouth, he saw that her teeth were too strikingly white and that none were missing, and this made him shudder; once again she split apart into images of two women, but he didn't want to admit it; he wanted to reunite them by force and violence, and so said: 'Don't you really feel like having some cognac?' When with a charming smile and a mildly raised eyebrow she shook her head, he went behind the screen, took out the bottle, put it to his lips, and took a swig. Then it occurred to him that she would be able to detect his secret action from his breath, and so he picked up two small glasses and the bottle and carried them into the room. Once more she shook her head. 'At least symbolically,' he said and filled both glasses. He clinked her glass and made a toast: 'This is to talking about you only in the present tense!' He downed his drink, and she moistened her lips. He took a seat on the arm of her chair and seized her hands.

# 10

She hadn't suspected when she had agreed to go to his bachelor apartment that it could come to *such* touching, and at first she had been struck by fright; as if touching had come before she had been able to prepare herself (the *state of permanent prepared-ness* that is familiar to the mature woman she had lost long ago; we should perhaps find in this fright something akin to the fright of a very young girl who has just been kissed for the first time, for if the young girl is *not yet* and she, the visitor, was *no longer* prepared, then this 'no longer' and 'not yet' are mysteriously related as the peculiarities of old age and childhood are related). Then he moved her from the armchair to the couch, clasped her to him, and stroked her whole body, and in his arms she felt formlessly soft (yes, soft, because her body had long ago lost the sensuality that had once ruled it, the sensuality that had endowed her muscles with the rhythm of tensing and relaxation and with the activity of a hundred delicate movements).

But the moment of fright quickly melted in his embrace, and she, very far from the beauty she had once been, now reverted, with dizzying speed, to being that woman, reverted to that woman's feelings and to her consciousness, and retrieved the old self-confidence of an erotically experienced woman, and because this was a self-confidence long unfelt, she felt it now more intensely than ever before; her body, which a short while before had still been surprised, fearful, passive, and soft, revived and responded now with its own caresses, and she felt the distinctness and adeptness of these caresses, and it filled her with happiness; these caresses, the way she put her face to his body, the delicate movements with which her torso answered his embrace – she found all this not like something learned, something she knew how to do and was now performing with cool satisfaction, but like something essentially *her own*, with which she merged in intoxication and exaltation as she found her own familiar continent (ah, the continent of beauty!), from which she had

33

been banished and to which she now returned in celebration.

Her son was now infinitely far away; when her host had clasped her, in a corner of her mind she caught sight of the boy warning her of the danger, but then he quickly disappeared, and there remained only she and the man who was stroking and embracing her. But when he placed his lips on her lips and tried to open her mouth with his tongue, everything changed: she woke up. She firmly clenched her teeth (she felt her denture pressed against the roof of her mouth, she felt that her mouth had been filled), and she gently pushed him away, saying: 'No. Really, please, I'd rather not.'

When he kept on insisting, she held him by the wrists and repeated her refusal; then she said (it was hard for her to speak, but she knew that she must speak if she wanted him to obey her) that it was too late for them to make love; she reminded him of her age, if they did make love he would be disgusted with her and she would feel wretched about it, because what he had told her about the two of them was for her immensely beautiful and important. Her body was mortal and wasted, but she now knew that of it there still remained something incorporeal, something like the glow that shines even after a star has burned out; it didn't matter that she was growing old if her youth remained intact, present within another being. 'You've erected a monument to me within your memory. We cannot allow it to be destroyed. Please understand me,' she said, warding him off. 'Don't let it happen. No, don't let it happen!'

# 11

He assured her that she was still beautiful, that
in fact nothing had changed, that a human being
always remains the same, but he knew that he was
deceiving her and that she was right: he was well
aware of his physical supersensitivity, his increas-
ing fastidiousness about the external defects of a
woman's body, which in recent years had driven
him to ever younger and therefore, as he bitterly
realised, also ever emptier and stupider women;
yes, there was no doubt about it: if he got her to
make love it would end in disgust, and this disgust
would then splatter with mud not only the present,
but also the image of the beloved woman of long
ago, an image cherished like a jewel in his memory.

He knew all this, but only intellectually, and the
intellect meant nothing in the face of this desire,
which knew only one thing: the woman he had
thought of as unattainable and elusive for fifteen
years was here; at last he could see her in broad

daylight, at last he might discern from her body of today what her body had been like then, from her face of today what her face had been like then. Finally he might read the unimaginable expression on her face while making love.

He clasped her shoulders and looked into her eyes: 'Don't fight me. It's absurd to fight me.'

# 12

But she shook her head, because she knew that it wasn't absurd for her to refuse him; she knew men and their approach to the female body; she was aware that in love even the most passionate idealism will not rid the body's surface of its terrible, basic importance; it is true that she still had a nice figure, which had preserved its original proportions, and especially in her clothes she looked quite youthful; but she knew that when she undressed she would expose the wrinkles in her neck, the long scar from stomach surgery ten years before.

And just as the consciousness of her present physical appearance, which she had forgotten a short while before, returned to her, so there arose from the street below (until now, this room had seemed to her safely high above her life) the anxieties of the morning; they were filling the room, they were alighting on the prints behind glass, on the armchair, on the table, on the empty coffee cup – and her son's face dominated their procession; when she caught sight of it, she blushed and fled somewhere deep inside herself; foolishly she had been on the point of wishing to escape from the path he had assigned to her and which she had trodden up to now with a smile and words of enthusiasm; she had been on the point of wishing (at least for a moment) to escape, and now she must obediently return and admit that it was the only path suitable for her. Her son's face was so derisive that, in shame, she felt herself growing smaller and smaller before him until, humiliated, she turned into the mere scar on her stomach.

Her host held her by the shoulders and once again repeated: 'It's absurd for you to fight me,' and she shook her head, but quite mechanically, because what she was seeing was not her host but the face of her son-enemy, whom she hated the more the smaller and the more humiliated she felt. She heard him reproaching her about the cancelled grave, and now, from the chaos of her memory, illogically there surged forth the sentence she had shouted at his face with rage: *The old dead must make room for the young dead, my boy!*

# 13

He didn't have the slightest doubt that this would
actually end in disgust, for even now the look he
fixed on her (a searching and penetrating look) was
not free from a certain disgust, but the curious thing
was that he didn't mind; on the contrary, it aroused
him and goaded him on as if he were wishing for
this disgust: the desire for coition approached the
desire for disgust; the desire to read on her body
what he had for so long been unable to know min-
gled with the desire immediately to soil the newly
deciphered secret.

Where did this passion come from? Whether he
realised it or not, a unique opportunity was present-
ing itself: to him his visitor embodied everything
that he had never had, that had escaped him, that
he had missed, everything that by its absence made
his present age intolerable, with his thinning hair,
his dismally meager balance sheet; and he, whether
he realised it or only vaguely suspected it, could

now strip all these pleasures that had been denied him of their significance and colour (for it was precisely their terrific colourfulness that made his life so sadly colourless), he could reveal that they were worthless, that they were only appearances doomed to destruction, that they were only metamorphosed dust; he could take revenge upon them, demean them, destroy them.

'Don't fight me,' he repeated as he tried to draw her close.

Before her eyes she still saw her son's derisive face, and when now her host drew her to him by force she said, 'Please, leave me alone for a minute,' and she escaped his embrace; she didn't want to interrupt what was racing through her head: the old dead must make room for the young dead and monuments were useless, even her monument, which this man beside her had honored for fifteen years in his thoughts, was useless, all monuments were useless. That is what she silently said to her son. And with vengeful delight she watched his contorted face and heard him shout: 'You never talked like this before, Mother!' Of course she knew that she had never spoken like this, but this moment was filled with a light, under which everything became quite different.

There was no reason why she should give preference to monuments over life; her own monument had a single meaning for her: that at this moment she could abuse it for the sake of her disparaged body; the man who was sitting beside her appealed to her; he was young and very likely (almost certainly) he was the last man who would appeal to her and whom, at the same time, she could have, and that alone was important; if he then became disgusted with her and destroyed her monument in his thoughts, it made no difference because her monument was outside her, just as his thoughts and memory were outside her, and everything that was outside her made no difference. 'You never talked like this before, Mother!' She heard her son's cry, but she paid no attention to him. She was smiling.

'You're right, why should I fight you?' she said quietly, and she got up. Then she slowly began to unbutton her dress. Evening was still a long way off. This time the room was filled with light.

This story was first published in English in the short-story collection *Laughable Loves*. That original volume contained an introduction by Philip Roth, who singled out this story as one of Kundera's best:

'Kundera's amusement emerges as a kind of detached Chekhovian tenderness in the story about the balding, thirtyish, would-have-been eroticist, who sets about to seduce an ageing woman whose body he expects to find disgusting, a seduction undertaken to revenge himself upon his own stubborn phallic daydreams. Narrated alternately from the point of view of the thirty-five-year-old seducer and the fifty-year-old seduced, and with a striking air of candor that borders somehow on impropriety – as though a discreet acquaintance were suddenly letting us in on sexual secrets both seamy and true – this story, "Let the Old Dead Make Room for the Young Dead", seems to me "Chekhovian" not merely because of its tone, or its concern with the painful and touching consequences of time passing and old selves dying, but because it is so very good.'

Philip Roth, 1974